CAN
RUN AND JUMP

81

KNOWLEDGE BOOKS

MASTERY DECODABLES

Tas is a cat.

She can run and jump.

She can play and sit.

The mat is her toy.

The mat is her bed.

Tas is my pet.

She likes apples and eggs.

Tas likes a pat and her mat.

She likes me.

Tas is so good and kind.

She is so little.

Her nose is so little.

Her tail is little.

Her arms are little.

Her legs are little.

But her eyes are so big.

Tas likes to play, play, play.

Tas likes to run, run, run.

She likes to sit.

She is so happy.